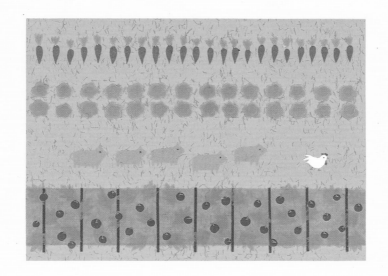

CUCKOOBUSH
FARM

To my parents
from Kazuko

Text copyright © 1987 by Dick King-Smith
Illustrations copyright © 1987 by Kazuko
First published in Great Britain in 1987 by Orchard Books
All rights reserved. No part of this book may be reproduced or
utilized in any form or by any means, electronic or mechanical,
including photocopying, recording or by any information storage
and retrieval system, without permission in writing from the
Publisher, Greenwillow Books, a division of William Morrow
& Company, Inc., 105 Madison Avenue, New York, N.Y. 10016.
Printed in Belgium   First American Edition   1 2 3 4 5

Library of Congress Cataloging-in-Publication Data
King-Smith, Dick.   Cuckoobush Farm.
Summary: Each season brings new things to see and
do on the farm as Hazel enjoys the newborn animals.
[1. Farm life—Fiction. 2. Domestic animals—
Infancy—Fiction] I. Kazuko, ill. II. Title.
PZ7.K5893Cu 1987   [E]   87-14871
ISBN 0-688-07680-7   ISBN 0-688-07681-5 (lib. bdg.)

CUCKOOBUSH
FARM

Story by DICK KING-SMITH

Pictures by KAZUKO

It is springtime at Cuckoobush Farm.
   There are baby birds in their nests, baby
rabbits in their burrows and newborn lambs
in the field.

The swallows are back and, from a bush in the wood behind the farm, the first robin sings.

After milking, Mr Meadows the farmer and
his dog, Gyp, drive the cows back to the field.

The speckled hen has hatched a brood of
chicks and there are ducklings on the pond.
Mrs Meadows and Hazel feed them.
 ''I do love babies,'' says Hazel.

Jack works on the farm with Mr Meadows. He plows and harrows the field ready to sow the spring barley.

In the next field Hazel counts the lambs as
they play around their mothers.
"The more the merrier!" says Hazel.

It's early summer at Cuckoobush Farm.
  Mr Meadows and Jack have loaded the hay
bales on to the trailer. Hazel and Gyp go
along for the ride, sitting on the bales.

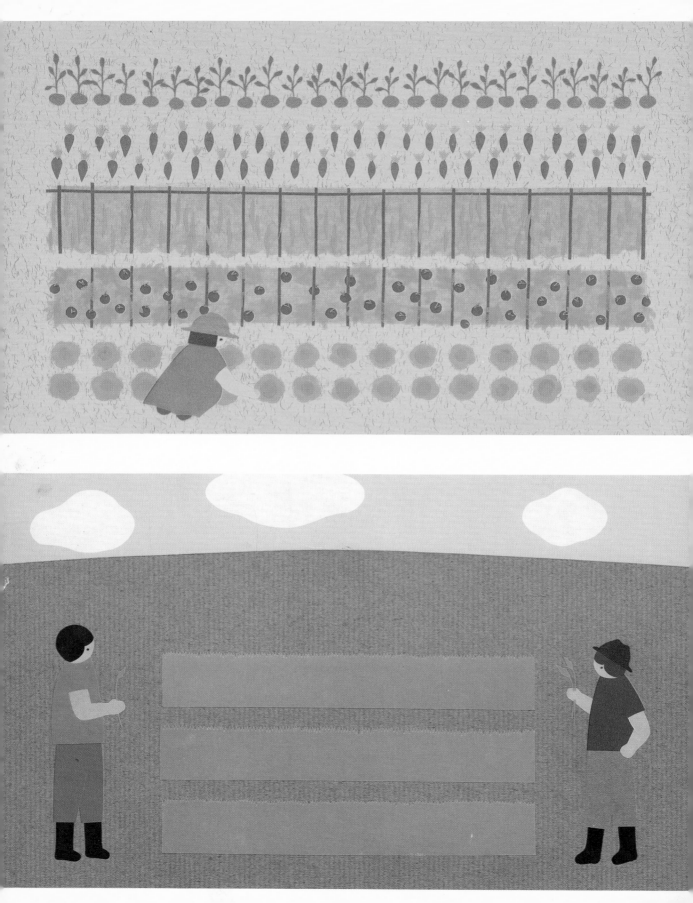

Mrs Meadows spends a lot of time working in
her vegetable garden.
   She grows carrots, cabbages, potatoes,
tomatoes and beans.
   Mr Meadows grows barley and wheat.
Hazel grows sunflowers.

Summer is almost over.
  Hazel and Gyp look at the sheep and count
them to make sure they are all there.

The barley is ripe and Mr Meadows cuts it
with the combine. Jack follows him around
the field with a tractor and trailer, and the
combine shoots the grain into the trailer.

Late in the afternoon Mr Meadows and Hazel
drive the cows into the shed for milking.

Gertrude the pig has had a litter of piglets.
Hazel counts how many there are.
"I do love babies," says Hazel.
"The more the merrier!" says Mrs Meadows.

It is autumn at Cuckoobush Farm. The swallows are flying south for the winter.

Jack plows a field and sows winter wheat.
He has put up a scarecrow to frighten away the
crows, but they still come and peck at the seeds.
Hazel stands in the field too, pretending to
be a scarecrow.

Jack has put away the combine, the tractor and trailer, the harrow and the plow for the winter.

Mr Meadows is feeding the new calves, born this autumn.

"What a lot!" says Hazel, counting them.

"The more the merrier!" says Mr Meadows.

"I do love babies," says Hazel.

"Good," says Mr Meadows, "because at Christmas you're going to have a baby brother or sister."

Winter is here. All the animals are snug. The cows are in the covered yard, the sheep are in a little sheltered paddock, and Gertrude the pig is fast asleep on a nice bed of straw in her sty. Her babies have grown big and gone to market.

Jack is sawing logs.
  Hazel feeds the hens, but the wild birds are
hungry too.

Now it is Christmas Day. Snow is falling.
Hazel is building a big snowman when
Mr Meadows comes out of the house.

"You've got a new baby brother *and* a new baby sister!" he says.

"The more the merrier!" shouts Hazel and she rushes indoors to see them.

It is almost the end of winter at Cuckoobush Farm. Lambing has started again.

Every night before she goes to bed Hazel is allowed to go out to the lambing shed and see how many lambs have been born.

She doesn't notice the hungry fox slinking
through the farmyard.

Now it is spring again at Cuckoobush Farm. The swallows are back and, from a bush in the wood behind the farm, the first robin sings.

Hazel is a whole year older, and now she
has the twins to look after...

as well as the calves, the chicks, the piglets,
the ducklings and the lambs.
    ''It's a good thing that I do love babies,''
says Hazel.

89-29745

E
Kin

King-Smith, Dick
Cuckoobush Farm
513327

89-29745

E
Kin

King-Smith, Dick
Cuckoobush Farm
513327